where did that naughty little hamster go?

by Patty Wolcott
illustrated by
Rosekrans Hoffman

J. B. Lippincott   New York

*"To all children
who are learning to read"*

by Patty Wolcott
Beware of a Very Hungry Fox
The Cake Story
The Forest Fire
I'm Going to New York to Visit the Queen
The Marvelous Mud Washing Machine
My Shadow and I
Pickle Pickle Pickle Juice
Super Sam and the Salad Garden
Tunafish Sandwiches
Where Did That Naughty Little Hamster Go?

First published by Addison-Wesley Publishing Company
Where Did That Naughty Little Hamster Go?
Text copyright © 1974 by Patty Wolcott Berger
Illustrations copyright © 1974 by Rosekrans Hoffman

Library of Congress Cataloging in Publication Data
Wolcott, Patty.
  Where did that naughty little hamster go?

  Summary: A group of first graders search the class-
room for their missing hamster.
  1. Children's stories, American.   [1. Hamsters—
Fiction.   2. Schools—Fiction]   I. Hoffman, Rosekrans,
ill.   II. Title.
PZ7.W8185Wh 1985   [E]   84-40796
ISBN 0-201-14245-7

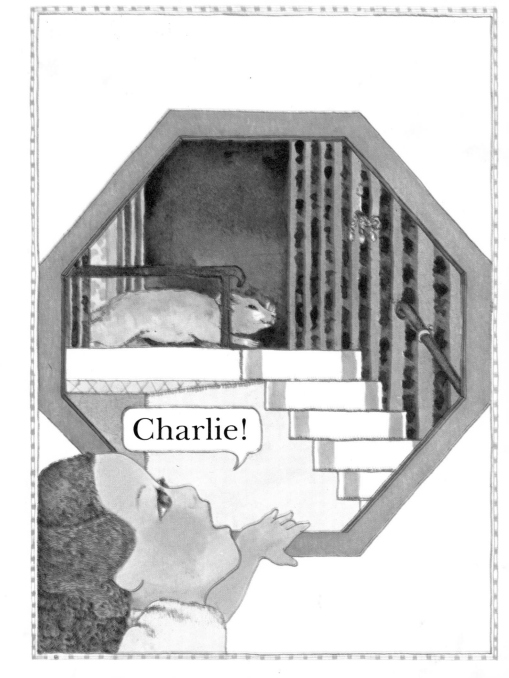

Charlie Hamster!

That naughty hamster!

CLOTH SCRAPS

Dear little Charlie Hamster.